This book belongs to

Patrick.

All love.

Granny Lizzie &
Grandpa Rich

For the people of the
Luangwa Valley, Zambia and
their own Wonky Tusk.
With love M.G.

For Leo and Ellie.
With love K.G.

First published in the UK in 2008 by Muddy Boots,
Fryer's yard, 2, Holly Tree Cottages, Cock Lane, Elham CT4 6TL

Text and Illustrations copyright © Meg Griffiths 2008

Design by Zero Design Ltd.

ISBN-13 978-0-9560719-0-3

Printed by Scotprint in Haddington, Scotland.

Wonky Tusk

Meg Griffiths

illustrated by Kate Gooding

Mum and Dad gazed down at their new baby son. Would he have wonky old tusks like the rest of the family?

"Can you *see* a tusk yet?" the baby elephant asked, morning, noon and evening.

He waited and he waited but, as there was no sign of a tusk appearing, he started being a naughty little elephant.

The little elephant sat fanning
himself with a large palm frond.
It was very hot and he was thinking
hard. When he thought a lot, he
often found naughty things to do.

He loved frightening the guests
from the nearby safari lodge.
That was always good fun.

And yesterday he had seen a new wall being built at the lodge which just might have been made out of sugar cane. He decided to check it out for his lunch.

He had eaten only half of the bamboo wall,
when a frightened guest started screaming,
pulling up her knickers and running for the door.

The baby elephant trumpeted gleefully.
The day had started off very well indeed.

"I hear the sound of water",
said the little elephant, flapping his
very large ears and covering himself
in red dust.

" I hear the sound of splashing water", he said.
His long trunk was twitching with excitement.

Oh yes, the guests were having fun in a pool of blue water!

Time to be very naughty, he thought, rushing towards the water and the frightened guests, who all leapt out of the pool in a great hurry.

" This is going to be such a good game!" thought the naughty little elephant, as he filled his trunk with water...

... and ran around the pool, trumpeting with laughter and squirting water all over the place.

But, before you could say "wonky tusk", the water had all gone and the little elephant stared into the empty pool in great disappointment.

" There's no water to swim in", said the little elephant to his friends.

"And no one to play with either". The guests showed no sign of coming back for a game.

Out of the corner of his eye, the little
elephant saw a large green hosepipe.
He dragged it to the side of the pool.
He would fill the pool up again!

But the hose began to move. It developed a
nasty spitting tongue and a black, beady eye.

"Snake!", shouted the little elephant.

"Nasty, hissing snake!" he trumpeted.

"Nasty, hissing, striking snake!" he bellowed, as the guests looked on from the safety of the lodge.

The little elephant then settled himself down under a palm tree, in the evening shade. He sat thoughtfully chewing on an old bit of sugar cane.

At that moment a monkey started chattering excitedly from a nearby tree. He pointed to the little elephant who looked down his trunk to see... a small but very wonky tusk! Perhaps I should be a good little elephant now, he thought.

That is, of course, until the pool had been filled up again and the "hose" had disappeared up a drainpipe.

Wonky Tusk

Muddy Boots